For my readers.

Without you, this Christmas tale wouldn't have been told.

LITTLE WHITE Christmas

J. Lynn Bailey

ONE

Sarah Beth

It was this day in particular that Sarah Beth loved most. November 30.

It wasn't because it was the last day of November, but because it was the night before the best month of the year.

Even at twenty-seven years old, Sarah Beth couldn't contain her excitement for December 1. She loved Christmas and all that led up to it.

"A little to the left, Sarah Beth," Josie Tuckett said.

From the ladder, Sarah Beth moved the wreath just a smidgen to the left, holding the giant Christmas wreath up against the glass. She saw her breath in the form of a white cloud.

Oh dear. Oh no, Sarah Beth thought. *This is much too cold for November 30.*

Nerves started to build in her belly. The colder weather usually started on December 12 or December 13 depending on when leap year fell. Sarah Beth knew something horrible was about to happen.

"Josie, do you see that?" Sarah Beth asked, staring down at her best friend from atop the ladder.

Josie looked from side to side. "See what?"

"Your breath," she huffed. "It's too early to get this cold." Sarah Beth stared down Main Street, first to the left and then to the right.

Josie laughed. Rolled her eyes. She loved Sarah Beth dearly, but sometimes, her superstitious ways were a little too unconventional.

Bad luck to wish someone happy birthday before the big day, to have facing mirrors because it opened up a doorway to hell, to go straight home after a funeral.

In fact, after Don Brockmeyer's funeral, Sarah Beth had driven around the block eighteen times before she drove Josie home.

And you never slept with your head to the east.

But seeing one's breath in the cold was a new one, even for Sarah Beth.

"What's it mean?" Josie asked as Sarah Beth hung the wreath above the door at Book Ends, Josie's own cozy little bookstore that she'd paid for all on her own.

"How should I know? But it can't be good though. Something bad's about to happen, Josie. I can feel it in my toes." Sarah Beth climbed down off the ladder and looked back to admire their work.

The Dillon Creek Chamber of Commerce started the Christmas music at five o'clock on the dot, as planned, which played out of tiny speakers that traced down Main Street.

Josie smiled.

Sarah Beth tried to allow the Christmas music to fill up her insides and take away the pit of doom she felt in her belly.

"Shit," Josie said.

And just as she'd started to believe that Sarah Beth might be wrong about the cold weather on November 30, she took it all back in just one glance.

Josie took her friend by the arm. "Let's go inside, where it's colder—warmer. I mean, warmer."

Maybe Sarah Beth was right after all.

Could Josie have seen a ghost from the past?

Could she have seen the only thing that would most likely put her friend back into a tailspin?

Tailspin, Josie thought, *might be too strong of a word. A frazzle perhaps. A disturbance.*

Oh dear. This isn't going to be good. Not in the least.

Josie stood in front of the big, heavy glass door that welcomed readers in the summer and kept them warm in the winter. As much as Josie tried to turn Sarah Beth away from the door, it was no use.

"Josie, what are you doing? What is goin—" But Sarah Beth's words fell short.

Josie could pinpoint the moment Shane Sawyer walked past her shop just by the look on her best friend's face. What gave it away most, however, was her mouth, which fell open, just like Toby Lemon's pants on New Year's Eve. Every single year, in the most creative way possible, he'd try to use Cranky Carl's planter boxes out front of the Blacksmith Shop as a commode.

Josie also had never seen Sarah Beth's eyes grow so big in her life. Not since they'd met in kindergarten.

Not even when they'd both caught Ms. Shields, their sixth-grade teacher, and Mr. Poolman in the janitor's closet.

Not when rumors had spread about Anna and Colt.

Not even when Mr. Pine had died right in front of them at Wilson's Grocery.

No, Sarah Beth's eyes were something different.

Sadder.

Angrier.

Vengeful maybe.

Shane Sawyer was taller than most cowboys—Sarah Beth was convinced it was the cowboy hat that made him look even taller. But at that moment, she could see only that night. That night when he'd come home for a few days exactly two summers ago.

Sarah Beth had known his track record, his way of operating. He was a sly dog. An extremely handsome, sly dog who had money and the fame that went along with being a top cowboy in the National Finals Rodeo for a few years.

She knew all of this before he ravaged her in the church that night.

A church of all places.

In God's house.

And if sex in God's house wasn't superstitious enough, well then, she'd write her own book on that subject.

Sarah Beth knew she was going to hell the instant he laid her down on the floor, between the pews, before God and angels and the souls of past parishioners.

She'd also known she'd let it happen.

Sarah Beth had just gotten the principal job at Dillon Creek Elementary since Principal Brown didn't work out. Turns out pending lawsuits didn't sit well with the district. Sarah Beth had been excited, and she and Josie had gone to The Whiskey Barrel for a drink to celebrate.

"Sarah Beth, say something. Right now. Show me you can breathe. Something," she heard Josie say.

But when Sarah Beth left her thoughts, she realized she was staring back at Shane in the window.

Josie took Sarah Beth's cheeks in her hands. "Sarah Beth!"

"That's why it's so cold tonight," Sarah Beth whispered.

She dropped her eyes from Shane, her best attempt to brush off his stare, and he disappeared into the night air.

Josie let go her hands from her friend's face. "Sarah Beth, if a heart attack doesn't kill you when we're eighty, hypertension from unneeded stress will."

"Did you know he was coming back into town?" Sarah Beth asked, her mind spinning.

Josie's eyes grew shifty. "Well, maybe. Delveen might have let it slip at church the other day. That woman knows everything before it hits the rumor mill."

Sarah Beth walked to the window to make sure Shane was gone. "She is the rumor mill, Josie." She turned back to her friend. "How come you didn't tell me?"

"Oh, so you could stress about it? And what if he didn't come back to town? I'd have told you for no good reason." She paused. "Not on your life."

"At least I could have had Pixie give me a quick color or something."

"Why do you care what Shane thinks? I'm pretty sure you said it was just a fling and that he didn't matter." Josie walked behind the counter. She knew better. Her friend had told her one thing, but her actions had told her another.

Sarah Beth had been heartbroken when Shane left.

"He doesn't. But after you sleep with a man, you still want him to find you just as attractive as he did before you had sex."

"You're lying."

"About what?" Sarah Beth looked out the window once more. Then, she opened the front door, grabbed some garland, and started to climb back up the ladder again.

The Christmas music filled her soul. The holidays always did. But something ticked like a time bomb in her chest, and she knew it was Shane.

"You still like him. And to be honest, I think you've had a thing for him since we were kids."

Sarah Beth gave Josie *the look*. "I did not and do not."

It was true. She did like him, and when he'd left with a quick note that said, *Had a great time. See you around* ... well, her heart had hurt for months afterward. She didn't tell anyone. She kept Shane locked inside her heart and only allowed herself moments with the memories when she was alone. The truth was, Sarah Beth was probably better off without a cowboy who had been destined to break her heart from the beginning.

Josie knew. After all, she was her best friend.

After Shane had left, Josie had filled her arms with romance and nonfiction books. Romance for the rush of it all, for the make-believe world readers could partake in, and nonfiction, well, because it was thought-provoking. It had been Josie's attempt at mending her best friend's heart.

"Come on. Help me hang this," she said to Josie.

"Promise me something," Josie said as she backed up from the ladder.

"What's that?"

"Don't let Shane ruin your favorite time of the year, all right?"

In that moment, Sarah Beth prayed that she wouldn't allow Shane to ruin Christmas. That she'd be kind if she had to be.

"It was just sex, right?" Sarah Beth tried to laugh it off.

At that exact moment, Erla Brockmeyer and Clyda Atwood walked by.

"Oh, hey, Mrs. Brockmeyer. Mrs. Atwood," Josie squeaked, clearly embarrassed. She bit down on her knuckle as both matriarchs smiled.

"We were young once, too, you know, girls," Clyda said.

Once both women were out of earshot, they said in unison, "It was just sex."

They both laughed.

Sarah Beth hung the garland.

Josie gave her directions.

The Christmas music played.

And Christmas lights lit up Main Street and Sarah Beth's heart. Maybe everything would be all right.

Sarah Beth couldn't sleep, so she came in to work extra early. Tess wasn't at school anymore because of budgets and seniority, which made Sara Beth's blood boil, so she invested her time in figuring out ways to bring her friend back to Dillon Creek Elementary. A loophole. Or some sort of oversight that had been missed. Overlooked.

It was easier perhaps for Sarah Beth to immerse herself in her work than field questions from her parents about finding a man to marry.

"Are you a lesbian, Sarah Beth?" her mother asked one night at dinner.

"Maybe," Sarah Beth said. Just because it was easier.

Sarah Beth wasn't a lesbian. She did know that. She had friends— Erin and Dora—who were lesbians, and she'd asked them questions before drawing a conclusion. Although it might be easier to be with a woman emotionally, she liked men.

"It's okay if you are. Your father and I just need to plan accordingly," her mother finished.

Sarah Beth wasn't sure what "plan accordingly" meant, but she was certain it involved preparing for no grandchildren.

"We need to talk to Charlie," her mother said to her father.

Charlie was indeed actually gay. But he hadn't come out yet. Sarah Beth wasn't going to be the one to tell her parents either. But she'd be there to support him, like she always had.

Sarah Beth fired up her computer and began to dig through the teaching contracts for each teacher.

If she couldn't figure out her heart, at least she could figure out clues to better decision-making at Dillon Creek Elementary.

Her father had said she should have been an attorney.

But the truth was, she loved kids.

And someday, she wanted a family of her own.

At noon, Sarah Beth walked uptown to grab a quick bite to eat. While walking, she was distracted by an email she was reading on her phone.

Never a good combination.

She hit something extremely hard, which was wearing a plaid button-up shirt and a cowboy hat.

"Christ," she whispered under her breath and tried to find the right words. "Oh, hey, Shane. I didn't know you were back in town."

One thing he didn't wear was a less than genuine personality.

Don't fall for his lean jaw.

His big green eyes.

His arms.

His long legs.

Jesus, Sarah Beth, breathe.

He was quiet for a moment. "Wasn't that you in the window at Book Ends? You were in Josie's shop, weren't you?"

Sarah Beth lied, "No. Nope. That wasn't me. Must have been someone else. Anyway"—her heart throbbed against her chest, her hands beginning to sweat, as she casually walked past Shane Sawyer—"I'd say it was good to see you, but—" *Oh God. Had she just said the but part?*

Sarah Beth tried to look past his green eyes. His sun-kissed skin.

It's winter, for God's sake, she thought. *Can't he be pale?*

His arm, however, was in a sling.

Don't you dare ask him how his shoulder is. It will show you might somehow care.

The National Finals Rodeo had just happened last week.

The whole town watched.

Shane Sawyer wasn't just representing the Sawyer family, but he was also representing Dillon Creek.

He went down on a steer at what looked to be the right time. But instead of getting the steer's head where it needed to be, the steer jerked his head back, taking Shane's shoulder with him.

When Shane lay on the arena floor, Sarah Beth held her breath and asked God to take away the sick feeling she felt in her stomach. And then she did what she knew how to do best—she turned off the television.

She couldn't watch.

Besides, it was easier not to know. Wasn't it?

Two seconds later, she flipped it back on just in time to see Shane being carried off with help from another cowboy in the arena.

Well, at least he lived, *she thought, her heart giving an extra beat.*

"Sarah Beth?" Shane asked. "Are you all right?"

TWO

Shane

Don't stare, Shane, you idiot, and keep the conversation light.
He liked when Sarah Beth did this. It was like he could watch a whole conversation take place in her head just by watching her facial features.

"Are you all right?"

"Just fine. Why wouldn't I be?"

Shane shrugged.

God, she's so beautiful, and she has no idea just how beautiful, he thought to himself as she pushed a strand of her hair from her eyes.

"I don't know."

Shane had spent years watching Sarah Beth Dawson. Since they were kids. Preteens. Teens. And now, adults.

"Good-bye, Shane," she said and walked past him.

In elementary school, Shane had secretly watched her do the next day's homework at recess as he played any sport with a ball.

He'd secretly watched as she quietly gave the longest explanation ever in the third grade about Newton's third law of motion.

He'd secretly watched when Danny Walker asked her to prom. And semiformal. And the homecoming dance.

He'd secretly watched as Sarah Beth slipped out of his grasp and left for college.

And when she'd left, Shane had told himself that he didn't deserve a smart, nice girl like Sarah Beth.

That the stars were aligned for him to become a rodeo star, so he could fulfill the commitment his father couldn't quite do, especially after Shane's mom died.

Shane was damn good at steer wrestling. He was good on a horse, quick. He had a keen awareness of his surroundings. And maybe he hadn't moved out of Sarah Beth's way as she stared down at her phone and walked.

Maybe he'd wanted her to run into him.

He thought, *it doesn't matter.*

He was certain she hated him for leaving. But she'd made it clear that the church was a one-night deal only.

Shane had tried to blame it on the booze, what had given him the gumption that night to finally approach Sarah Beth.

Why'd she make him so nervous? Shane had been with women. Plenty of women, and for that, he'd probably given himself a reputation. But when it came to Sarah Beth, he panicked. He always faltered. Lost for words. His palms always grew sweaty.

"Slogger! It's so good to have you back in town, man! I mean, I'm sorry to hear about your shoulder, but it's real good to see you," Lance Belotti, an old dairyman and one of his father's friends, slapped him on the back.

Some of the old cowboys had nicknamed him Slogger because of Shane's work ethic. If he wasn't on a horse— herding cattle, mending fence, bucking hay, branding, or working on his steer wrestling—one would find him helping another cowboy or mowing someone's lawn in town. Shane didn't take too well to sitting on his hands. Besides, his dad was half-drunk all the time anyway, so someone had to pick up the slack where he couldn't.

"Thank you, Mr. Belotti."

His father had trained him with manners.

"When do you think you'll head back to the circuit?"

"Soon as possible," Shane said.

If Shane didn't work, he didn't make money. He wished he could say it was for the passion of the sport, but when all the cards were on the table, it was the only thing Shane did well.

He hadn't gone to college.

Barely finished high school.

Besides, Dillon Creek had gotten too small for him.

"Well, you take care of that injury, you hear? Don't go back too soon."

"No, sir."

Lance slapped his back once more and continued down Main Street toward his truck.

Shane got into his truck, but when he looked in the rearview mirror, he saw Sarah Beth walking across the street, most likely back to the elementary school.

Go ask her if she needs a ride.

A small pinch of confidence made him start the truck.

Shane quickly opened the slider window in the cab of his truck and threw a few beer cans back there. He couldn't remember when he'd drunk those or how long they'd been there.

He flipped around, put his foot on the gas, and headed toward Sarah Beth.

She was a block away from the school when Shane caught up to her.

His stomach was in knots when he tried to casually rest his elbow on the frame of the window. "Need a ride, Sarah Beth?" Shane's heart slammed against his chest. Hammered. Jackknifed somewhere between *ride* and *Sarah.*

"No, thank you, Shane."

Just when Shane built up a bit of courage to ask Sarah Beth to lunch, Tilly Puckett, daughter of Tony and Pixie Puckett, leaned in the other window. "Hey, handsome. Heard you were back in town." She opened the truck door and hopped in.

No.

Shane looked from Tilly back to Sarah Beth, but she was already gone.

Tilly Puckett was good for his ego. She stroked it, and he enjoyed that. But that was all there was to it. Besides, as much as he'd tried to forget about Sarah Beth, he simply couldn't. She'd ruined his sex life with all other women. Every time he allowed himself the pleasure of another woman, all he could see was Sarah Beth's face.

Tilly Puckett was no different, but he wasn't going to sleep with her. Besides, he'd gone down that lane with her before. Shane didn't need a rumor following him around like they used to. He wasn't that guy anymore.

Am I?

"Anyway, I don't know why you came back here, Shane. Nothing's changed. Same people. Same gossip. You ought to get gone and stay gone. I mean"—she smiled and used her fingers to climb up his arm—"I'm glad you're here. Real glad."

"Look, Tilly, I just can't."

"What do you mean, you can't? Somethin' broke?" She looked down between Shane's legs.

"No, nothing like that. Just …" Shane didn't need to explain anything. He pulled the truck over in front of Tilly's house.

She pouted and crossed her arms across her chest. "You used to be a damn good time, Shane Sawyer." Tilly climbed out of the truck. "Who broke you? Was it that damn Sarah Beth?"

Shane smiled. "Bye, Tilly."

"Asshole," he heard her mutter under her breath before she slammed the truck door.

Later that night, Shane sat down at the table with his father, Jack.

Shane's mom, Corrine, had died when he was ten. But one thing he remembered most about his mother was that she'd loved the holidays. She'd decorate the house with garland, lights, and small, traditional knickknacks from her side of the family. She'd make cookies, breads, and candy. It seemed like Christmas music played from the first of November to New Year's Eve. And Dad never settled on a mediocre Christmas tree. It had to be the biggest, most perfect tree from Sandy Ale's lot up off of Grizzly Bluff Road.

But Christmas just hadn't been the same since his mom passed on December 4 seventeen years ago.

Dad hadn't either.

He'd retreated into himself.

Drank to numb the pain.

And somehow, Shane just kept moving forward. He guessed that was a big part of why he hated the holidays.

Jack never put up a tree again.

The house never smelled like Mom's cookies.

She'd left a big hole when she passed. A hole in Dad, a hole in Shane, and a hole in the ranch.

"Got to get that shoulder healed," Jack said.

"I know."

"Got to get back into that arena," Jack said. Sipped his beer.

It had always been his father's dream to do the rodeo circuit, not Shane's. Shane just happened to be good at it. But because he'd done it for so long, he'd developed a deep love for the sport.

"You're a natural," his father always said.

"Put in a call to Eureka Orthopedics. Dr. Mason owes me a favor. Broke his gelding last year. Said he could get you in."

In truth, Shane had gone to the emergency room per the National Finals Rodeo doctors, but he'd left before he went in. Maybe Shane was scared of what they'd tell him. Rodeo was his life.

Maybe, he thought, *I can give it time to heal and then have a surgeon doctor look at it.*

If he couldn't rodeo, especially at the level he was, then what the hell was he going to do?

Shane also knew if he went back to the circuit, he was certain the next time he came home, Sarah Beth would be married and pregnant with another man's child.

Was he willing to risk that?

"I think you need to have Dr. Mason take a good look at it."

"Yeah, all right. When?" Shane matched his father swig for swig of their beers.

"Tomorrow morning. I can drive you."

"No, I can drive myself." Shane knew his father would be up at the crack of dawn on a horse, moving hay, building fence, doing what old cowboys did at five in the morning. Shane also watched his father drink to chase away the memories of his mom. So, when he combined the two—work and alcohol—it just made his life survivable, and Shane didn't want to put a monkey wrench in that.

Shane still had the memories, too, and he didn't know what was more painful—having the memories or nothing at all.

"Night, Dad."

"Night, son."

Before Shane closed his eyes as he lay on top of his covers in his childhood room, he looked at the walls.

Posters of Lane Frost. Ty Murray. John Jones, Sr. Ote Berry. Chris LeDoux. George Strait, all heroes in Shane's eyes, rodeo kings and country singers.

He looked around the room at all the ribbons and the dusty belt buckles that sat on his dresser, untouched for years. The three saddles perched in his room on old wine barrels. It was true; there wasn't enough space in his room for his trophies, so his mom had made him take some out to the old milking barn. But the important ones stayed in his room, only to collect dust.

Shane wondered what it would be like if his mom were still here. Maybe he wouldn't worry about his dad so much. Though Jack was tougher than nails. Shane had seen his dad's jaw and leg and both arms broken, all separate occasions, all done by riding saddle bronc.

Maybe his dad wouldn't drink so much.

But, hell, he was an adult. Shane knew his dad would figure it out, but it didn't stop the worry.

He'd go to the doctor tomorrow, and they'd probably tell him that he was hurt real bad. Shane could feel it. He wasn't an idiot.

Shane dug around in his pocket for the white pill he'd grabbed earlier from his truck, popped it in his mouth, and swallowed it whole. He only took them when the pain got real bad. And the pain got real bad when he was lying in bed. At least it would take the edge off.

Hawthorn—Shane's travel buddy and hazer, who kept the steer from running astray and the only guy he trusted—had given him a bottle before he left for the emergency room.

Shane had tried to explain he could drive himself, but the rodeo officials, the doctors, wouldn't have it.

Just when the pain pill started to take effect, his cell phone sounded, signifying a text message.

It was Hawthorn.

Did you hear about Jimmy? Bull hooked him through his side. Not looking good, man. Just thought you needed to know.

There was a Professional Bull Riders event in Texas.

That was the thing about rodeo. Nothing was safe. Nothing was set in stone that said a cowboy would live to see another day. It was just the price cowboys paid for doing what they loved.

Whatever's going on with my shoulder is peanuts compared to Jimmy, he thought.

This thought made him sick. Or maybe it was the pain medication. But he got up anyway and walked out to the living room.

Dad was passed out in his chair, his beer between his legs.

Shane took the beer and moved it to the sofa table. Sat down on the couch.

His dad was watching a rerun of Shane steer wrestling. It was from a few years ago.

He'd won the finals that year. It was the fourth round. Two-point-eight seconds—that was what it took Shane to get the steer down.

The crowd screamed.

Shane's dad had sent him a picture of Veterans Hall at Dillon Creek, packed with cowboy, fans, and families, all watching him.

That was a good year.

The pain medication filled him with okayness. He thought about texting Hawthorn back, but he wouldn't have an update.

Jimmy has a wife and two kids.

He walked to the fridge to grab another beer. *This will help, at least momentarily.*

Shane opened it and took a big swig. Sat back down on the couch and let the video play through.

He started to think back on that year. The real good year when he had won a lot of events. He'd made quite a bit of money.

And yet, every year since, he kept trying to relive it even if it meant tearing up his body to achieve it.

The truth was, he hadn't had that kind of real success since.

He wasn't so sure he ever would again.

Shane put the bottle to his lips, leaned back, and watched the video over and over until he finally fell asleep.

Maybe he'd done everything so impeccably well that ride that maybe it was just something he was missing now.

But maybe Shane's time had passed—on a few different fronts.

THREE

The Ladybugs

The Ladybugs were a group of old ladies who gathered at Dillon Creek Pizza on the last Tuesday of the month at noon sharp to raise money for scholarships for kids and the community. They were quite picky about who their members were. But if the group wanted to be sustained over the years, it needed to recruit new members. Get them trained. Hell, The Ladybugs weren't getting any younger.

And in order to make any group work for as long as they had, there had to be roles they played well. The group had to possess these types of people: one leader who took charge—Clyda Atwood; a person who could see all sides to the story—Erla Brockmeyer; the easygoing one but would do anything it took to meet the needs of the group—Mabe Muldoon; a gossip to get the lead on any good thing in Dillon Creek, and in the case of the Ladybugs, they had two—Delveen Constance and Pearl Harvey.

Erla had just lost her husband in July, so the group pulled her weight because her cheese, most days, had been sliding off her cracker. She hadn't gone crazy; it was grief—and an ugly dose of it. So, in reality, The Ladybugs had four proper working minds for the moment.

"Well, I heard he got a rodeo groupie pregnant in Texas a few months back," Delveen disclosed before their meeting began.

It was unclear how Delveen and Pearl seemed to get access to rumors and gossip so quickly, but the group had to admit, it did have its perks in a small town.

It gave the group access to halls before they were booked. Such was the case with The Purple Scarf Society. Their president, Lucille, and three other board members had been caught playing poker in the good Lord's house one night while Pastor Mike and his wife, Frances, were out of town. It was a scandal. Anyhow, The Purple Scarf Society had booked the Veterans Hall for a gathering on a date that The Ladybugs also wanted the hall. Delveen said to keep the date booked at the hall for next in line. So, they did.

Lo and behold, after the poker scandal had broken, The Purple Scarf Society had backed out, and the Ladybugs had been able to rent the hall instead.

One would think, however, that after all these years, Clyda Atwood wouldn't be so surprised by Delveen and Pearl and what came from their mouths, but she was. "How do you know Shane Sawyer got someone pregnant in Texas?" Clyda asked.

"Travis Hawthorn's mama," Delveen said matter-of-factly.

"Oh shit, Delveen, that woman's got one foot in the grave," Mabe said.

Then, Delveen replied, "Mark my words, someone's going to show up to our town of Dillon Creek with a cute little belly with the Sawyer baby in tow." She pushed her salad around her plate.

Clyda shook her head in doubt.

Erla tried to smile.

Mabe finished her nonalcoholic beer.

And Pearl checked her lipstick with the reflection of a knife.

Some things never changed, except when drama came to town.

FOUR

It wasn't like Sarah Beth had lied. No, well, maybe she had. But in her defense, she couldn't help the way she responded to Shane's presence. She was always lost for words. It burned her up, too, that he could do that to her. She had seen him in the Book Ends window that night.

After spending the day wiping noses, calling parents, working on budgets, and trying to dig up anything to get Tess's job back, Sarah Beth was tired.

Her phone chimed in her purse.

It was a text from Josie.

Where are you? It's the town Christmas tree lighting tonight. Thought we were going to meet at the shop at 5?

Oh no. She looked down at her phone. It was already five fifteen p.m., and it started at five thirty.

She texted back.

On my way.

Sarah Beth and Josie had a yearly ritual that they'd done for years. With Shane back in town and with work, she'd completely forgotten all about it. Sarah Beth had promised herself she wouldn't let Shane take away her love of the holidays, and here she was, forgetting about life.

She turned off the light to her office. She was always the last one to leave.

Leaders should be, she thought to herself.

She buttoned up her wool coat, put on her knitted gloves, tucked her purse under her arm, and made her exit from the school. She took a right and then a sharp left to Main.

Christmas music played.

The lampposts were lit up with lights snaking down them—a reflection of tradition of Dillon Creek, the carefulness of preservation. After all, the lampposts had been a stamp on Dillon Creek since they were erected in 1901. Each storefront, even Cranky Carl's Blacksmith Shop, took to decorating their shop windows for the holidays. While there was money at stake—the business that won first prize took home one hundred dollars, second prize took home fifty dollars, and third prize took home twenty-five dollars—it was more about the parking. The first-place winner got to park on Main Street for the entire year. Typically, business owners weren't supposed to park on Main Street, as they allowed for tourists to have those highly sought-after spots. And also, bragging rights.

But on that night, the air was cold. The storefronts looked magical, and Sarah Beth couldn't help but feel as though everything was as it should be.

Even if Shane Sawyer was in town.

Frank Sinatra's "Have Yourself a Merry Little Christmas" came over the airway.

Sarah Beth dodged every crack in the sidewalk.

She pulled her coat around her even tighter, as if she could.

But he slipped into her head, just like he always did.

She was twenty-seven. Why hadn't she settled down yet? Was she subconsciously waiting for Mr. Perfect? Sure, she'd been on dates—some not-so-pleasant ones, some okay ones. But truth be told, maybe she was looking for someone who was unavailable. Someone who didn't exist.

She remembered when Shane's mom had passed away.

The whole town mourned.

Just like they had when Tripp and Conroy were killed.

And when Don Brockmeyer died.

And when John and Francine Muldoon died.

But she felt particularly sad when Shane's mom died. She saw it in his eyes. The once-bright green eyes full of hope and a zest for life had somehow become vacant, less available, hopeless even.

That was when Shane made the move from being a boy to a man overnight. He turned to things to fill the void in his heart. Sarah Beth saw it; just like a light switch, Shane turned everything off. It wasn't like he turned into an awful kid. His dad, Jack Sawyer, an old cowboy, wouldn't let that happen. Shane just hadn't seemed to care anymore.

Sarah Beth wondered what he was doing tonight. She couldn't help it when she pulled open the big glass door to Book Ends. It smelled lovely. Pine and sugar cookies.

It was 5:22 p.m.

"I'm so sorry," Sarah Beth explained as the door shut behind her, and she looked up.

Josie had decorated the inside of Book Ends. It had always been their tradition to decorate the storefront but never on the inside. It looked like a winter wonderland. As Sarah Beth pulled off her coat, she looked around at the garland and the big Christmas tree that stood in the middle of the store, standing ten feet high. The white flakes of plastic snow sat on ledges, bookshelves, and countertops.

She stared at her friend in awe. "This is beautiful. How on earth did you get the Christmas tree in here by yourself?"

"Tom Manzel," Josie said shyly, as if she was hiding a secret crush that Sarah Beth was completely unaware of. And she was.

Oh. Have I been so completely wrapped up in my own saga that I couldn't see that my best friend has feelings for a new man?

Josie changed the subject. "Do you like it?"

"Oh, Josie." She swung her arm around her best friend. "I love it. It's perfect." She led Josie over to the warm mugs of cocoa, and they added a little peppermint liquor to them. "So, tell me more about Tom."

Josie blushed. "I don't know what there is to say. He wandered in here one day, looking for a book. We got to talking. Then, I asked him if he'd help with the Christmas tree."

Sarah Beth took a sip of her cocoa. "Did he ask you out?"

Josie smiled. "He did."

"And?"

She frowned. "I told him no."

Sarah Beth froze. "Why did you tell him no? Tom is a great guy. Has his own construction business. Loves dogs. You've got to love a man who loves dogs."

"I don't know. I panicked. I mean, he's divorced. What if … what if he has some weird fetish? Or some quirky habit— or more than one quirky habit? Or more than one fetish?" Josie's face turned bright red. It did that when she was nervous.

Sarah Beth laughed. Josie had always been a *worst-case scenario* person.

"And some people just grow apart." Sarah Beth paused for a moment. "Trust your heart, Josie. What's your heart say?"

"Well …" She thought on it. "I'm having trouble deciphering my undeniable physical attraction to him and the potential long-term relationship—if, of course, he doesn't indeed have a weird fetish or habits. I suppose my heart says I should take him up on his offer."

"Worst-case scenario, it doesn't work out, right?" Sarah Beth took another small sip of her cocoa.

"Yes, but then I'll see him around town. And then it will be super awkward. And then the whole town will know we were dating and then we're not, and everyone will feel the awkwardness."

"But we'll all go on."

"True."

"I say, take him up on his offer."

"Yeah, okay. I think I will."

They clanked their mugs together, giggled, and talked some more.

"Seen Shane around town?"

Sarah Beth couldn't help but roll her eyes. "Saw Tilly slither into his truck, like the snake she is."

"Oh, someone seems jealous."

Was it jealousy that Sarah Beth felt? Or was it pent-up resentment from the time she caught her then-boyfriend, Danny Walker, and Tilly snuggled up in a closet one night at a party?

"Disdain," she answered.

"What was Shane's reaction?"

Sarah Beth thought about it. "I don't know. I guess I was so caught up in her that I didn't pay attention."

"Just my two cents based on experience, but sometimes, we're so focused on the bad that we can't see the good."

Sarah Beth inhaled her best friend's wise words.

Perhaps she's right, she thought.

"Come on. Let's go watch our little ol' town light up," Josie said, sticking the liquor and the mugs beneath the counter.

The town gathered around the impressive one-hundred-and-fifty-foot spruce tree at the end of Main Street, decorated by the Dillon Creek Volunteer Fire Department. Homemade cookies had been made by the Scout troops, and music was provided by the Booster Band.

Christmas in Dillon Creek truly was magical.

Mayor Dupont began. "Always a tradition to gather among friends and family to watch the annual Christmas tree lighting since 1934 ..." he began.

Sarah Beth scanned the crowd.

Tom squeezed through the people to get closer to Josie and her. "Mind if I stand with you?"

Josie grinned. "Not at all. Also, I'd like to take you up on that date—if you're still available, that is," she said quietly.

Tom smiled real big. "I'd really like that."

Josie nodded. "Okay then, it's decided."

Sarah Beth grinned, trying her best not to eavesdrop but she couldn't help it.

And there, next to Jack Sawyer, stood Shane. And he was staring right at her.

A chill pushed through Sarah Beth's body. One that made her toes tingle, her fingers vibrate, and her heart exceed the normal amount of beats per minute, which would surely kill her if it continued this way.

But instead of allowing the resentment in, she smiled at Shane Sawyer, and every inch of her body felt it when he smiled back.

Neither of them could deny the moment or take away any felt feelings, shared memories, or stolen glances from across the play yard as kids. It felt different for Sarah Beth. Different in a sort of way that made Christmas miracles.

The question wasn't if she cared deeply for him because that had started as kids, and she knew it now. The question was, when he left again—because he would since he was a cowboy with a need and passion for what he did—would he come back? Would she be willing to settle for a part-time lover? And could she trust that when he was on the road, he'd remember her? That he wouldn't forget the girl from home who'd loved him since kindergarten?

Sarah Beth wasn't so sure she was willing to risk the heartbreak for a few months of good love. The safest way she experienced life was to always play on the cautious side of things. Less risk. Less damage for all parties involved.

The Booster Band started to play "We Wish You a Merry Christmas," which took Sarah Beth from her thoughts and transported her back home, to the heart of where beautiful things always seemed to start—at Christmastime.

Once the song stopped, the town did the countdown, and the giant spruce lit up.

A hush of awe fell over the residents of Dillon Creek. It really was a sight to behold.

Sarah Beth looked over at Shane to witness his reaction, but instead of looking up at the tree, he was staring straight at her.

Something about Shane made her nervous and excited all at the same time, just as it always had since they were kids. Maybe it was his way with the women of Dillon Creek—and perhaps women all over the United States—with his smoldering green eyes, broad shoulders, and his ability to talk a woman out of her pants in five seconds flat.

She'd seen it happen in high school. Not so much as adults, as he'd been gone for far too long. But she knew the Tillys of the world climbed all over him, and he willingly allowed it.

She stared back at Shane, a smile no longer touching her lips. Doubt and insecurity danced in her mind and in her heart.

Maybe Shane wasn't worth the impending heartbreak. He'd done it once already.

But a quiet voice inside Sarah Beth said, *Maybe you never really let the real him in, in the first place.*

The crowd began to disperse.

And before Josie, Tom, and Sarah Beth made their way back to Book Ends, Tilly Puckett pushed herself alongside Shane, as if some sort of participation award. But this time, Sarah Beth paid attention to Shane's reaction. It wasn't the look Shane had given Sarah Beth inside the church as he pushed inside her. Taken her mouth and given her what she'd asked for. It wasn't the look she felt in her bones and ran from, for fear of heartbreak. No, not at all. Shane stared only at Sarah Beth, and it was as if he was begging her for just a few stolen moments of her time.

Maybe, just maybe, she could give that to him.

FIVE

Shane

Shane tried not to approach Sarah Beth that night even though he wanted to. No, he lingered on the outskirts of the people she spoke with. He wanted to know if her skin felt the same way he remembered it and if she still smelled like lilacs and oranges. If she still talked the way she talked behind closed doors when she was turned on. Shane had really enjoyed that. He wanted to know if she remembered the way he'd made her feel that night and what she'd said afterward.

The words that had ripped out his heart.

Tilly Puckett moved to Shane's side. But he couldn't peel his eyes from Sarah Beth. He wanted Sarah Beth to see he wasn't interested in Tilly Puckett. Annoyed, he turned his body away from her, toward his dad, toward Lance Belotti and Rue Samuels, who were talking cattle.

"It's almost like you don't remember two summers ago, Shane," Tilly whispered in his ear.

He would have rather forgotten. It was a night out at The Whiskey Barrel with Hawthorn and some of the guys from the circuit, and he'd had way too much to drink. That was also before Sarah Beth.

"Look, Tilly, I'm trying to be as nice as possible, but I'm not sure how you're going to take the hint. I'm not into you, and there's no way we're going to have sex."

Tilly smiled. She was persistent. "You say that now, Shane, but you'll be back." With that, she walked away.

Shane knew to his core that he wouldn't dare mess anything up with Sarah Beth ever again even if he had to wait out his entire adult life for her to come around, but he also didn't need to explain that to anyone.

He looked back to find Sarah Beth, but she was no longer there.

He searched the crowd for her. *Just one last look,* he told himself, so he could take her memory home and tuck it into his dreams.

But she was nowhere to be found.

Shane's heart started to jackhammer in his chest. Sarah Beth was the only woman on this earth who could make his heart do things like that. A sense of urgency came over him. If he didn't tell Sarah Beth how he felt, she'd move on. She'd have a husband by June and be pregnant not long after.

It was clear to Shane at that instant that if he didn't make the move now, while he had the guts, he'd never do it. With that information spilling over in his head, he quickly walked down Main Street and noticed her wool jacket.

He ran, and his shoulder began to throb.

Josie and Tom were with her.

He caught up to them.

"Sarah Beth," he said breathlessly. "Just a minute of your time?" he asked.

Josie touched Sarah Beth's arm. "Tom's going to walk me home. Call me later?"

Sarah Beth nodded.

Tom shook Shane's hand.

And then they left Sarah Beth and Shane standing on Main Street below the wreaths on the lampposts, below the twinkling Christmas lights, beneath the sky that Shane was sure would cave if Sarah Beth said no to his proposal.

His mouth felt dry, and his heart was pounding. He let out a big breath, took off his cowboy hat, and ran his fingers through his hair. In that moment, he convinced himself that if he got tongue-tied again or allowed his fear of heartbreak to overcome him, he'd be risking everything.

So, he started slowly and tried to pace himself. "I'd like to clear the air between us, Sarah Beth. I'd like to take you to dinner, if that's all right with you. Just so we can talk."

Shane wasn't going to profess his love to her right out here among the stars and the moon or anyone walking by. Sure, it seemed romantic. And it wasn't that he was embarrassed or ashamed. He was worried for Sarah Beth. He didn't want to catch her off guard. Unprepared.

He could see the trepidation in her eyes. The sadness she hid so well. The sadness that only people who loved Sarah Beth could see.

"Just give me an hour. Tomorrow night. And if you still never want anything to do with me, I'll understand. But I can't leave Dillon Creek, Sarah Beth, until you know how I feel."

The furrow in Sarah Beth's eyebrows, the one that reflected the sadness, softened somewhat, and Shane saw it as an opportunity. "Please."

She thought about it.

The Christmas music still played.

He wished Christmas were over already, so everyone could get on with their lives.

"What time?" she whispered.

"Six? I'll pick you up."

Sarah Beth agreed.

Shane nodded and smiled, his heart that night grew a little freer and a little less lonely and a whole lot sweeter.

"Can I walk you home?" he asked when she finally turned to leave.

"No."

Shane nodded again. "You sure?"

Sarah Beth stopped. Turned back to face Shane. "Why?"

And then this came from his mouth. It wasn't planned. It wasn't thought out. It was just there. And somewhere deep inside, he thought his mom had something to do with it. "The way I see it, our days are numbered, and time will eventually run out. Our bodies will be no more. But if I can spend just two more minutes of this life with you that I didn't have yesterday, well then, that's two minutes that I didn't have before."

Sarah Beth's face changed. Shane could tell she was trying not to smile, as if her heart was hardened from life, like a protective shield had been built around it. He understood all too well.

"All right, Shane Sawyer."

He walked her home that night in the cool temperatures of winter and under the bright white stars and the moon that seemed to smile down on them, as if the universe trailed behind them, giving them the okay to fall in love.

Shane watched her as she avoided all the cracks in the sidewalk.

"Why do you do that?" he asked. He knew she'd done it since they were kids. He'd just never asked why.

"Come on, Shane. You can't tell me that you don't do some weird ritual before you go wrestle a thousand-pound steer."

Shane laughed. Thought on that for a minute. "Suppose I do. I, uh … say a prayer and shove a feather in my boot for good luck."

"Step on a crack, break your mother's back," she recited.

The tension eased between them as they left their memories behind them.

They reached her front door.

Shane stood back for two reasons. One, he didn't want to make Sarah Beth feel pressured to kiss him, though he'd be lying if he said he didn't want to kiss her. And two, he wanted to marvel at the beautiful woman, whom he'd loved since they were kids, in the moonlight.

"Were the two minutes worth it?" she asked as she opened her front door.

Absolutely nobody ever had to lock their door in Dillon Creek.

"Yes," Shane said breathlessly in the cold night air.

And then she said, "What happened to Shane? What happened to the guy who wore the shield and who didn't care about the world around him?"

Shane thought. "You."

And with that, Sarah Beth smiled once again. Nodded. "Good night, Shane."

"Night, Sarah Beth."

She quietly and slowly shut the front door.

Shane walked back to Main Street to get his truck. It was the first time in his life that he'd felt content since his mom died. He'd spent years trying to fill holes in his heart with metaphorical bandages, short-term fixes that would last an hour, maybe two. But for the first time, Shane felt free and full and as if everything was right where it should be.

He wasn't sure what tomorrow held for them or the next day or the next. He knew he'd have to figure out the balance of rodeo life and his personal life. But one thing was for sure; if Sarah Beth would have him, he'd move mountains to keep her.

Shane and his dad mended fence until dark. With one hand, he was still a big help to his dad. It made him think of how his dad had done all of this on his own while Shane was gone on the circuit, chasing women and doing whatever the hell he felt like.

"Who helps you when I'm not around?" he asked his dad.

Jack pulled some wire cutters from his back pocket. "No one."

Shane stopped. Stood from his crouching position.

"I mean, Lance and Bo would come over if I asked, but I'd hate to ask them," Jack said. Clipped a wire. "Look, you have the skill and the ability that I sure as hell never had at your age.

You are on the right path. Don't worry about me. Your goal is to stay at the top. Rodeo is your life, son. Go be great."

Shane was never one to argue with his dad. But with these conversations they'd been having lately, nothing felt right.

Leaving for the circuit again.

Leaving his dad.

Leaving Dillon Creek.

Leaving Sarah Beth.

All of it.

Dad was getting older, and he would work—mending fence, breaking horses, bucking hay, and running a ranch that was way too big for him—until he couldn't anymore. And even then, to a cowboy, that meant his body had to be buried in the ground before he gave up on the ranch.

They both went inside.

Shane showered and came out, dressed in a long-sleeved blue-plaid button-up shirt, Wranglers, and his going-to-town boots. He put his cowboy hat on when he reached the door and grabbed his jacket.

"Where are you headed off to?" Jack asked.

"Dinner."

"A date?"

"No, dinner."

"A date?" Jack smiled. "Sarah Beth?"

Shane paused. He'd never in his life mentioned Sarah Beth to his dad. "How'd you know?"

His dad took another sip of his beer from his recliner. "I've always seen the way you look at her. Reminds me of the way I used to look at your mother. Have a good time, son."

His father always had a way of knowing. Observant to a fault. Shane remembered, as a kid, he'd watch his dad. Jack would study the bucking horses at rodeos, the cowboys that rode them well, make notes on a little notepad that he kept in his breast pocket.

One day, Shane had asked him why he took notes, why he watched others so intently.

Jack's answer had been simple. "If you're not watching, you're not learning."

"See you tonight," Shane said.

"See you tonight," his dad said.

Shane made his way to town, but he parked on Main Street instead of Sarah Beth's house, so he could steal a few more minutes with her.

He made the two-minute walk from Main to her house.

And when she answered the door, his words left him. The pang in his heart made his chest shudder.

An angel stood in front of him and wore a red sweater that went to her thighs, black leggings, and cowboy boots. Her hair was down around her shoulders, and her milky-white skin glowed.

"Well, you clean up nice, cowboy."

But Shane didn't answer. He couldn't.

"Did you walk here?" Sarah Beth shut the door behind her.

"Can I help you with your coat?" Shane finally said as they made their way to town.

"Sure." Sarah Beth handed him her coat.

And when he went to take it from her, his good hand grazed hers. Sparks illuminated in his heart. He hadn't touched Sarah Beth in two long years, and he still remembered what she'd felt like. Dreamed about it.

The way each of her breasts filled his mouth.

The way they tasted.

The way his hands looked against her hips as he held her against him and pushed.

And when their chests united, he'd thought he'd die in the feeling it gave him.

Shane tried to act casual, but when her scent—lilacs and oranges—collided with the memories of that night, he knew he didn't stand a chance of normalcy or anything that went along with subtle.

Just when they began to walk again, Shane's phone chimed in his back pocket. "Sorry, I meant to put that on silent."

Sarah Beth shook her head. "It's fine."

Just as they turned the corner, Sarah Beth asked how his day had been.

In that moment, Shane realized he could spend a lifetime with Sarah Beth. It wasn't just in the way she'd asked him, but he could hear the sincerity and the love in her voice. A type of love that got stuck in someone's heart and never left.

Shane's phone chimed again. He sighed and pulled his phone from his pocket. Just as he went to flip it to silent, he saw the text from Hawthorn.

Jimmy didn't make it.

SIX

Sarah Beth

S hane hadn't needed to tell her that she looked beautiful. She could tell by his reaction. The way his chest had paused and he held his breath and for all the words he didn't say.

But when Shane looked down at his phone, she knew something was terribly wrong.

"What is it?" she asked.

Shane was stoic. She watched his face as he tried to search for what to say.

"Shane?" She placed a hand on his good shoulder and felt a need to hold him in her arms, but she refrained. "Are you all right?"

Shane took his eyes from his phone to her face. "Um … a good friend died."

Sarah Beth never reacted, not that she didn't want to, but she rarely did. She pulled Shane to her and held him. "I'm so sorry, Shane." She allowed his scent to take her back to that night. She allowed his body to touch hers. Allowed his heart to hurt against her chest.

Sarah Beth even stood on a crack in the sidewalk as she hugged him.

Shane didn't cry.

He didn't say anything.

He didn't move.

But she felt the weight of his body. "We don't have to go to dinner."

"No, we don't have to, but I'd like to," he whispered.

The combination of the cold outside and his warm breath against her neck sent chills down her spine.

They walked in silence to The Whiskey Barrel, and her hand fell in his by accident—or not by accident because maybe she did want her hand in his. They grabbed a quiet corner table next to the window that overlooked Main Street. Sarah Beth noticed Christmas music played softly in the background.

The waitress, new to Dillon Creek because Sarah Beth didn't recognize her, took their food and drink order. She arrived back with a beer for Shane and a glass of house red for Sarah Beth.

Amid the sadness, Sarah Beth couldn't help but enjoy the Christmas decor in The Whiskey Barrel. Mavis Morgan had excellent taste. Whether it was Saint Patrick's Day, Easter, or Christmas, her decor was always on point. And truth be told, maybe it wasn't that Sarah Beth enjoyed only the atmosphere but also the company that she kept on this cold winter night even if the weight of silence was heavy.

"Can you tell me about him?" Sarah Beth asked. She touched Shane's good hand that rested on the table. Sarah Beth had learned that it was sometimes easier to talk about it than to hold it all in.

"He had a wife and two kids. He loved riding bulls but loved his family more. Did it to pay the bills." Shane let out a deep breath. "Listen, Sarah Beth, I need to tell you something."

Sarah Beth took a sip of her wine. Swallowed a touch of fear that she'd somehow found.

"If I don't tell you now, I never will." He begrudgingly removed his hand from hers, finished his beer, and stared at her from across the table. Smiled as if he'd found a memory he had tucked away in his heart for some time.

"What is it, Shane?" Sarah Beth tried to prepare herself, as she always did.

"I'm convinced now"—he smiled, burrowed his eyes into hers, and it made Sarah Beth blush—"that I've loved you since we were kids, and I love you today."

This wasn't what Sarah Beth had expected. In fact, it caught her off guard, yet it touched her heart in all the right places, created warm spots in places she had felt nothing in a long, long time. She didn't say anything. She just listened and tried to hide the feeling Shane Sawyer gave her. A feeling no man had ever given her.

"And I'm afraid if I don't tell you this, I'm going to miss my opportunity at real love." Shane held his breath. Broke eye contact with her. Perhaps it was because of the vulnerability of the moment, the way he'd just exposed himself so raw. "Say something, Sarah Beth," he pleaded.

Don't look too eager, Sarah Beth told herself.

She breathed him in, his words, and tried her best not to melt. "When I was a little girl, my mother always said to wait for the man who made your heart double over itself. Wait for the man who saw your faults and loved you anyway. The man who treated you like you deserved. I fell for you the day I saw you stand up for little Lenny Warner, all four feet of him, when we were in the third grade. Do you remember?"

Shane didn't remember. Cocked his head to the right.

"It was right before your mom died. Gary Bovine and Ryan Carter had stuffed him in the trash. You'd walked around the corner just in time to see it all happen. And then you proceeded to let the two boys have it. Got suspended for it. And never told a soul that you'd defended a boy who was being bullied. And if I remember things correctly, I think Lenny, after your suspension, brought you his mom's homemade brownies for months afterward."

Shane smiled. Nodded. "I remember now. But I think what I remember the most was the brownies."

Sarah Beth paused when she saw Shane's smile. Tried to tread lightly on his heart before she said, "It was freshman year. I watched your life spin out of control with the partying, the girls. I thought, *How can I love a boy who loves other girls without care or with regard?* So, it was then and there that I told myself that I could never fall in love with a boy whose heart seemed broken from the start. But pieces of me—big pieces of me—couldn't help but want to take care of you. And then you changed. Everything about you changed because you became so reckless. And then I didn't feel the need to want to take care of you anymore."

The shame that covered Shane's face lay like a broken-in pair of jeans. It fit the crevices of the lines that ran the length of his face—well-earned heartbreak, she supposed.

"I made mistakes, Sarah Beth, some really poor choices, but you make me want to be a better person. And since that night we made love in First Christian Church, I can't forget about you. I've longed for you. I tried to ignore it, tried to push it under the rug, but I can't anymore."

Sarah Beth's words—the ones she had said after they had sex in the church, just to protect her heart—played in her mind over and over. Words that had come from a place of self-preservation and not love. "And then I said to you, 'It was just sex, Shane. I save lovemaking for those who can. I don't think you're capable.'"

"I am capable of love, Sarah Beth. And it's always been you. I'm scared if I don't tell you this now that you'll marry someone else and have two kids, and it will be the biggest step I never took because I was scared as hell of what you'd do and say."

"Why'd you run?"

He shrugged. "It was easier. I couldn't convince you I was in love with you that night. So, I tried to forget you. And I couldn't."

Sarah Beth said, "In love?" The words fell from her lips so carefully and so desperately.

The corners of Shane's mouth turned up. He nodded cautiously. "In love."

"I thought I was a number to add to the collection of women."

"There is no number, and there is no collection, Sarah Beth. And if that's what you thought, then … well, you've always been at the top, even before my lips touched yours."

Sarah Beth's breathing picked up pace. After she took a big sip of her wine, she set it down and stared at Shane square in the eyes. "Where do we go from here, Shane?"

"We eat," he said, and just as he said that, the waitress brought their food.

They both picked and thought and pushed their food around their plates. It wasn't that it wasn't divine; it was.

"My parents were older when they had me," Sarah Beth finally said. "My father fell extremely ill just after we made love in the church." Sarah Beth saw the crushed look on Shane's face. "I didn't tell you to make you feel bad. I told you because, that night, I'd made a choice. For the last two years, I blamed you for leaving. I blamed you for what happened between us. In truth, my decisions were my decisions. I'd made a choice that was reckless, yes, but I made it with a broken heart. I didn't mean what I said about you being unable to make love. I guess I just needed someone to hurt you as much as I was hurting. I saw the look on your face when we were done. The guilt. I didn't want to be your pity case. And now, I realize it wasn't that at all."

This time, Shane reached across the table and took Sarah Beth's hand.

The waitress returned. "How is everything? Can I get you anything else?"

"Just the bill," Shane said.

The waitress brought the bill.

Shane wouldn't take no for an answer as Sarah Beth attempted to pay for at least her portion.

The nip in the air was quite sharp as they left The Whiskey Barrel.

The wind whirled around them, cocooned them.

"I'll take you home in my truck," he said.

With his good arm, Shane opened the truck door for Sarah Beth, but before she climbed in, she kissed Shane on the cheek.

"I'm sorry." But the kiss she gave him wasn't meant to be sweet or soft. It was meant to be a token of passion and necessity.

They rode the thirty seconds it took to get to Sarah Beth's house.

Shane put his truck into the idle position, got out, went to her side of the truck, and opened the passenger door. He walked her up the walkway.

Sarah Beth wasn't nervous. Not this time. She was quite calm when she said, "Come inside?"

Shane looked at Sarah Beth. "Are you sure?"

"I haven't been surer of anything in an awfully long time, Shane."

Shane went back to his truck, turned it off, and let Sarah Beth lead him inside.

With the lights off inside and the wind howling, Sarah Beth guided Shane to her bedroom.

And then the rain began.

"I'm going to change. Are you comfortable?" Sarah Beth asked Shane.

"What are we doing in here, Sarah Beth?" He sighed as he gently touched the small of her back from behind.

"Making up for lost time," she simply said as his chest met her back. She felt his heart thumping. Her heart grew warm, as she knew she had this effect on Shane.

"I'm going to change my clothes," she said. "Get comfortable?"

Shane did and she slipped into the bathroom.

Sarah Beth stared back at the woman in the mirror behind the closed door. She stood tall and with a full heart. And she knew without a doubt that Shane was the one. And she also felt this tiny, tiny thought of trepidation, like something was on the horizon that was out of her control. Sarah Beth didn't know if it was good or bad, but she tucked it away and filed it with her old thoughts on Shane, not the new thoughts, the new feelings of Shane Sawyer.

And she'd always been one to trust her gut.

Without anything but a small silk robe slightly open, exposing her breasts, stomach, and thighs, she walked out into the dimly lit room.

The wind wailed.

The rain poured.

Shane's reaction to her made her feel like the most important thing in his life.

He walked to her, not cautiously, not with care, and stood in front of her. She felt his need for her. His breathing was labored. She could feel it against her breasts.

"God, Sarah Beth."

The longing look he gave her, she felt it in all the right places.

Her heart.

Her head.

And the ache between her legs.

"Make love to me, Shane?" she whispered meekly.

The ache only grew the second he stepped closer.

A low growl sounded beneath the layers of layers she'd just begun to peel back from his tough outer image.

Shane gently took off his sling. With his hands, he started just below her backside and slid them underneath her silk robe and up to her hips as he stared at her in the eyes.

She could feel him harden against her with just this single touch.

"We've got to take it slow, Sarah Beth." His voice was ragged already. "Because I'm not sure how long I'll last with you." He smiled against her mouth as he took hers.

He moved his hands to her jaw and kissed her, invited himself to explore her mouth with his tongue at first slowly and then with more urgency.

She pulled at his shirt as his hands moved to her shoulders and pushed the robe off.

Almost unwillingly, he stepped back from her to marvel at her body.

Sarah Beth stood there, her lips needing his, her body almost vibrating from his touch.

Shane stared at her and then at each inch of her body.

When he reached out and touched her breasts, she sighed, unable to control what came from her mouth.

She could tell that was too much for Shane, as he came back to her and picked her up with his one good arm. Sarah Beth wrapped her nakedness around him while he carried her to her bed.

He softly laid her down and stared down at her. He took his good hand this time and ran it down her stomach and then between her legs, barely touching her folds.

He unbuttoned his shirt as Sarah Beth watched. She saw the bulge in his jeans and so badly wanted to help him with that.

Finally, he slid off his jeans and his underwear, and she watched him climb on top of her.

He never once winced in pain.

"Does your shoulder hurt?" she asked.

Shane shook his head. But she knew better. It was the adrenaline of it all.

She'd never wanted another man more in her life.

He kissed her again. She pushed his back to the mattress and climbed on top of him, felt him between her legs. He smiled, and she did too.

He took a breast in his mouth, tugging gently on her nipple, which made her call out.

He laid her on her back and crawled between her legs. He spread them as he kissed his way down her stomach, to her folds. Gently, he took his fingers and exposed her.

"You're so wet, Sarah Beth."

She groaned. "That's what happens when you wait two years for the right guy to come along again."

He stopped. "You waited?"

"Yeah."

At first, he used the pad of his finger, touched her at the top of her folds, and moved.

Sarah Beth smiled and spread her legs further for him. She watched him watching her.

Then, he slid a finger inside her, and her body shuttered against the mattress.

"Again," she said.

He did what she'd asked. And then he took his tongue and flicked her warmth over and over and over until her hips moved and bucked.

"Please, I need you inside me."

But instead, he did things to her that night as the wind screamed and the rain made the world a different place outside in the darkness.

Sarah Beth waited for him to enter her, but he never did. He pleasured her over again.

She was certain he was uncomfortable with his shoulder and … in other ways.

"Why won't you make love to me?" she asked while she was in his arms, lying naked under the covers.

"Because I don't want you to think that's the only thing I want."

Sarah Beth sat up in bed and pulled the sheet to her breasts. "What on earth do you mean? I know that's not all you want."

He pulled her mouth to his and said against her lips. "I want you to know that I want your whole heart too."

And with that said, Sarah Beth climbed on top of him. Grabbed a condom from inside the nightstand.

Shane looked from the nightstand and back to her again. "I thought you said you hadn't—"

"A girl can never be too careful." She smiled, opened the condom with her teeth, and slid it down his length as he fell back against the pillow.

Sarah Beth sat directly above him and slowly eased herself on top of him.

Hard and ready, he pushed up from the mattress, and Sarah Beth felt all of him.

She moved with ease and precision as he stared hard at her, only to take her breast in his mouth once more. She watched him. He held her hips tightly to his as they moved together.

He was a broken little boy at one point, but now, he is a man, a powerful force to be reckoned with, with a stronger heart to follow, she thought.

In one swift movement, Shane lifted Sarah Beth from him, still with one arm, put her back to the mattress, and found her all over again. She could tell he needed to be in control, and she was okay with it.

She made sure he had full access to whatever he needed with her.

They climaxed together when the rain finally stopped.

Shane and Sarah Beth fell asleep in each other's arms, and they both knew their hearts belonged together, but there was yet another storm blowing into town that they didn't see coming. It was all just a matter of time.

SEVEN

Shane

Shane had never spent the night with a woman. Ever. He was a midnight runner. He'd always felt it was too intimate, and he'd never felt the need to.

But with Sarah Beth, he could stay forever.

So, when he woke up to the rain, the wind, and the slight light of morning, her naked body pressed to his, he thought it was all a dream.

He'd had this dream before—of being with Sarah Beth—and he always felt the empty feeling in the pit of his stomach when dawn would come and it was just him.

Shane tightened his arms around her, just to be sure things were real. He kissed her soft shoulder before he got up and went pee, washed his hands, and made coffee.

"Good morning," she said as she walked into the kitchen, the silk robe around her body.

Shane walked to her and kissed her for a moment. "Good morning. And if you don't stop wearing this robe, we will never make it out of this house."

"Nothing wrong with that, Mr. Sawyer. Besides, if you don't put a shirt on, I know we won't leave this house at least until Monday." She gave him one last kiss.

"How do you like your coffee?" he asked.

"Little bit of cream and sugar is fine, thank you."

Shane laughed to himself as he made her a cup.

"What?" she asked.

"This all feels like a dream." He looked at her and handed her a cup of coffee. "I actually had to kiss your shoulder this morning and make sure everything was real." He took a sip of his coffee.

Sarah Beth smiled, walked over to him, and rested her head on his back. Wrapped her arms around his middle. "Me too."

Shane adjusted himself so that she was against his chest. Kissed her head.

"How are you feeling with the whole Jimmy thing?"

"Not sure. I suppose I feel real bad for his wife and kids. Can't get them out of my head."

Sarah Beth, he knew, always had a soft spot for kids.

"Do you want kids, Sarah Beth?" he whispered in her ear.

"Yeah."

"Well"—Shane took Sarah Beth in his arms, and her legs wrapped around his middle—"let's go try and make some."

He kissed her on the mouth, and they spent the morning in bed, making up for lost time.

When Shane finally peeled himself from Sarah Beth's bed, he went home to take a cold shower, check on his dad, and make a few calls.

"Hawthorn, it's Shane. Call me when you get a minute." Shane left the message and clicked End.

He called the 1-800 florist number for the deal that always appeared in advertisements to send flowers to Natalie, Jimmy's wife, and his girls. Jimmy and his family lived down in Arroyo Grande, which was about six hours south of Dillon Creek. Each of them would receive a big bouquet.

From roses to peonies or daisies to lilies, he wasn't sure what to get, so when they asked him what type of flowers, all he said was, "The best kind that live the longest."

Shane texted Sarah Beth.

I love you.

Bubbles appeared on her end.

I love you.

He responded.

What's your favorite type of flower? Figured I should know this since we've already tried to make a baby together.

She texted back.

LOL. Dahlias.

This time, instead of calling the 1-800 number, he called Juniper at The Flowerpot and ordered twenty dahlias to be sent to Sarah Beth's house.

Then, he called Dr. Mason's office as a follow-up after the MRI. His shoulder hurt today. More than it had ever hurt before. But it was all well worth it.

"Shane," he sighed into the phone, "I have good news, and I have bad news."

Shane inhaled. "Give me the good first, Doc."

"The good news is, no surgery. The ligaments and tendons are stretched. But you're almost bone on bone. This isn't the first time this has happened, has it?"

Shane didn't answer.

He'd taken shoulder hits off fences with the horses. Running into steers with his shoulders was how he made his living.

He'd fallen off horses.

Endured several shots to his shoulders, and when the pain got to be too much, he'd ask for pain pills or a cortisone shot.

"A temporary bandage," the doctor had said. "You'd better get this looked at, Sawyer, before something real bad happens."

"Listen, from our conversation the other day, you can't continue to tear your body up because if you do, you will need surgery, and that could cause a lot of nerve damage, and you could potentially lose at least sixty percent of your shoulder mobility."

Shane had expected not-so-great news. But this kind of news took his breath from him. He'd always expected to have the choice between rodeo and walking away—not being forced to walk away from the only sport he excelled in.

"What are you saying, Doc?"

"I'm saying, you need to find a different line of work, Shane. If you don't, then you won't be able to do much of anything with that shoulder. No helping your dad on the ranch. Nothing."

Shane's words left him. He had so many questions, but he wasn't sure how to ask them. "Um, how long? How … how long until I'm healed?"

"At least six months, Shane. At the very least. You shouldn't be lifting anything. Moving anything."

Fuck that, he thought. He also knew he couldn't say that to the doctor who'd done his dad and him a favor. But he did say to himself, *I can't consider a different career, Doc. It's not in my blood.*

"Thank you," he said and hung up the phone.

Jack was standing in the doorway. "What'd he say?"

"Everything's fine. Just some strained ligaments and tendons. Be good as new in a few weeks. I can do what I need to help out here, he said," Shane lied.

He couldn't let his dad down. He knew how proud his dad was of him for making it as far as he had. Hell, he was twenty-seven years old. His body was still young.

"Help me with moving some hay today?" his dad asked.

"Yeah, no problem."

Later that day, Shane grabbed the last bale. His shoulder was in so much pain, but he pushed through. The agony made him work harder; perhaps it was his best attempt to prove Dr. Mason wrong.

"Cowboys never show weakness," his dad always told him.

Hell, Shane was sure the last time he'd cried was when his mom died, and even then, his dad hadn't. He told his son that crying wouldn't bring her back.

Once they were done for the evening, Shane grabbed a pain pill and got in the shower, allowing the hot water to run down his beaten body as he prayed the pain away.

His conscience chimed in, *You can't live like this, Shane. You can't live off pain pills and cortisone.*

But tonight, he could. He'd take Sarah Beth to dinner. He'd make love to her tonight and for as long as she'd have him. He had to get lost in something because life just seemed too overwhelming right now.

Shane's phone vibrated across his dresser. It was Hawthorn.

"Hey, man."

"Hey." Shane could hear the sadness in Hawthorn's voice. He wasn't in Dillon Creek, as he was still on the road, going to the next event. Hawthorn sighed, "Natalie doesn't want a service for Jimmy. She's too angry. You know where she was it with all the PBR shit. Felt like it was a death sentence."

Shane understood. Listened.

Although both of them were close to Jimmy, Hawthorn was closer. They were both married. Had kids. They had just a bit more in common than Shane.

Maybe, too, that was why Hawthorn was taking it harder.

And maybe, too, Shane was real good at pushing his feelings down. Too good. And because of that, he got better at hiding things and convincing himself if he didn't acknowledge them, then they didn't exist.

He heard a knock at the door, and his dad answered.

Who the hell would be here at six o'clock? Nobody ever came to the house unless he or his dad was expecting someone.

"I got to run, man, Keep in touch?"

"Roger that."

They hung up.

Shane threw on some clothes and walked into the living room.

A woman stood in the doorway. Her crystal-blue eyes stared past his dad and right at him. Eyes he'd seen before. Eyes he'd thought he'd left in the past. He knew they'd had sex, though his recollection fuzzy, but he didn't know her name.

"Shane Sawyer?"

"Yeah?" He walked up behind his dad.

"Can … can I help you?" Shane asked.

"Shane, we met in Texas about three months ago."

Yeah, he'd been in Texas three months ago.

And when Shane was able to see her whole body, he looked down at her swollen belly.

"Um, I just needed you to know … and I know this is really awkward, but I'm pregnant, and you're the father."

Time stopped.

And in that time, a loud ringing ensued.

Nothing could be heard.

Or seen.

Life was just frozen.

His gut wrenched.

And his heart slammed.

And this was nothing Shane wanted.

Oh God. Sarah Beth.

After Mia left—Shane hadn't known her name when she showed up on the porch—he texted Sarah Beth and told her he was on his way.

Shane had been careful. He wore a condom when sleeping with any woman. But it was a blur. He wasn't even sure it had even happened. But that was what you got with too much booze and painkillers. He'd come off a big win in Texas that night.

Panic filled his insides, his head included.

He needed to tell Sarah Beth the truth. He had to. Right? He couldn't lie to her. Not her.

Maybe he'd tell her in the morning when they woke up together in her bed. Maybe mornings were easier for news like that.

But the evening went by, and they made love that night.

They woke up the next morning, and Shane just hoped it had all been a bad dream and would go away.

He tried to forget about Mia.

"Let's go to The Rusty Nail for breakfast," Sarah Beth suggested.

Yes, Mia was mostly gone, on her way back from where she had come from, and maybe she'd find out that it wasn't his child after all. He'd explained to Mia that he wanted a paternity test as soon as possible. He didn't dare ask if she was going to keep it.

Regret and betrayal filled his heart when he climbed into the shower that morning with Sarah Beth.

They made love again. He touched her, and she touched him.

And this big secret sat between them.

He had to tell her.

I'll tell her after breakfast, he promised himself.

She deserved to know. Whatever the outcome, she had to know.

As they approached The Rusty Nail, Shane's arm around Sarah Beth, he knew in his heart that she was the only one for him.

Christmas lingered in the daytime like Christmas movie marathons.

It brought out the good and the bad in Shane.

It seemed to brighten Sarah Beth's spirit, and that was why he thought that maybe he ought to look at Christmas a little differently.

It was the tap on the shoulder that caught Shane off guard.

He turned with Sarah Beth under his arm.

It was Mia who stood before them.

EIGHT

The Ladybugs

"I heard the woman just walked right up to Sarah Beth and told her that she was having Shane's baby." Pearl took a bite of her salad with extra ranch. Shook her head. "Couldn't hear a damn word they were saying though. I've got to get these hearing aids fixed. But whatever words were exchanged, there wasn't much to it." She shrugged. "Sarah Beth just walked away. Shane tried to chase her, but she wasn't having any of it. Looked like she was more heartbroken than angry. But the audacity of that woman …"

"If that were my son, I'd make her marry that girl. Kids nowadays. Having babies out of wedlock and whatnot. Things never happened like that in our day," Delveen said. She took a bite of her salad, which was littered with pickled red beets.

But the Ladybugs grew real quiet when they saw Erla's reaction to the words that had fallen out of Delveen's mouth. It was subtle. Quiet. And yet so obvious. It was proven that Erla could drop a crow from the sky with just one look.

"I-I didn't mean—well, you know what I meant. Right, Erla?" Delveen looked at Erla, then to Pearl, and back to Erla.

Erla thought for a moment. The only man she'd ever loved, Don, had died. The man she'd had a child with, Toby, at a very young age and out of wedlock had caused a big rift between her and her daughter most recently.

"You mean, the baby I had out of wedlock, who Don raised as his own? Is that what you're talking about, Delveen?"

Everyone felt the condescending tone move across the table like thick honey.

And nobody answered Erla's rhetorical question. Truth be told, she probably wasn't expecting one.

"You know what I say to all this?" Erla pointed her bread at the other ladies at the table. "Hogwash. You don't know this woman's story, you don't know Sarah Beth's story, and you certainly don't know Shane's story, so butt out." Erla stuck her bread in her mouth, mostly so she wouldn't say something she'd regret.

They continued their lunch in silence. The Ladybugs hadn't planned on a meeting today because it wasn't the last Tuesday of the month at noon sharp. They were meeting about the Christmas auction, their annual fundraiser.

"Well," Pearl whispered, "wouldn't that be great if it wasn't his baby? Seems to me that Sarah Beth and Shane would be an awfully cute couple. I was reading an article the other day at the beauty shop, waiting for Pixie, about these DNA tests they do while the woman is still pregnant. Boy, that would have fixed a lot of those *Jerry Springer* shows, wouldn't it?"

"Not helping, Pearl," Clyda said.

Bless her heart, Pearl was just trying to be funny. She did have a kind spirit and a big mouth, but also a big heart. She wouldn't be a Ladybug if she didn't. But she always had awful timing. In lieu of trying to control what she might say next, she shoved a piece of bread in her mouth too. A big piece. To keep her quiet for a while. Bread was hard to eat with her dentures anyway, so maybe it would buy her at least ten more minutes.

NINE

Sarah Beth

Sarah Beth needed a hot bath and the dryer—a hot bath to drown the pieces of her broken heart and the dryer to disguise her cries and the ruckus that Shane was causing outside.

He pounded on her door for two hours before it stopped finally.

She poured herself a short glass of whiskey on the rocks. Sarah Beth wasn't a drinker. Sure, she'd had a few glasses of wine or cocoa with peppermint liquor here and there, but she didn't drink it for the head change. She drank it because she enjoyed the taste.

She never drank whiskey, and she definitely didn't drink it for the taste. And anyone who did drink it for the taste ought to be crazy.

But she needed two things that night: to unfeel the last twenty-four hours and to forget.

She knew this one would hit her harder than the last.

And so she buried herself in the hot water and bubbles and sipped and cried.

She knew it was against her better judgment—to date not just a cowboy, but also Shane Sawyer. She knew deep down in her heart that everything had aligned too perfectly.

How could I have been so stupid? she asked herself as tears began to pool in her eyes again.

Shane proved that an old dog couldn't learn new tricks.

She learned that a liar was always a liar.

Sarah Beth hadn't told a soul about what transpired today on Main Street. But she was certain that between God, the good folks of Dillon Creek, and nosy Pearl, the whole town was talking. It didn't matter.

She'd turned off her phone hours ago.

Sarah Beth held her whiskey glass to her lips and took long sip.

She choked.

She coughed.

She gagged.

And she did it all over again.

Sipped.

Choked.

Coughed.

Gagged.

The whiskey quickly slithered around her heart and head and allowed her toes to go numb and her fingers to tingle. While her throat still burned, her head felt lighter. The ache in her heart lessened.

She knew the madness of all of this would return tomorrow—along with a massive headache and a sour stomach.

Sarah Beth heard her front door jiggle.

 "Sarah Beth?"

She breathed a sigh of relief and sadness. "In here." Sarah Beth's voice broke.

Josie appeared in the doorway of the bathroom. "Are you wallowing?" she asked as she crossed her arms and leaned against the doorframe.

Josie had never been one to sit in self-pity, and neither would she allow her best friend the same luxury.

Sarah Beth said, "She's pregnant, Jo. Pregnant."

"Has a paternity test been taken?"

"It's not the fact that she's pregnant. It's the fact that he didn't have the balls to tell me the truth."

Josie walked to the toilet seat, put the lid down, and sat. "When did he find out?"

"I don't know."

"Is it his for sure?"

"I don't know."

"So, let me get this straight. This strange woman—according to Pearl because that's the version I heard—marched up to you both and told you she was pregnant with Shane's baby, and you didn't ask any questions?"

Well, since Josie put it like that, my reaction does seem a little premature, Sarah Beth thought.

"But he never said anything about a woman in Texas."

Josie let out a cackle. "How do you suppose he would have done that—or rather, when would he have done that? Hell, Sarah Beth, he was just winning you back. I can see why he'd wait. At the very least, give him a chance to share his side of things. You listened to the woman but didn't give Shane the opportunity to share his piece."

A single tear navigated its way down Sarah Beth's face. She wasn't sure she could take the truth. But she had to. She wanted to know. She needed to know the truth, just so she could move on with her life. "Suppose I hear him out, then what?"

"Well then, you know. Then, and only then, can you make a logical decision. Because, right now, best friend, you're running on booze and a broken heart, and those two are never a good combination." She picked up Sarah Beth's glass from the lip of the bath and smelled it. "Oh God. Whiskey? Has it really come to this?"

"It was the only thing I had under the sink."

"Well, I'd rather drink dish soap." Josie made a face.

Josie, Sarah Beth knew, would always give her the truth, no matter how bad or how dire the situation. And that was something she admired most about her best friend. Because, in the end, she was always there to help Sarah Beth pick up the pieces.

"Tell you what. I'll give you until tomorrow morning to wallow. After that, you're going to call Shane, and you're going to ask for his side of things. Then, you'll make a choice." Josie stood. Kissed her friend on the forehead. "Come on. I'll help you get in bed."

Josie helped Sarah Beth out of the bath. She was a little tipsy, laughing one minute and crying the next.

When Josie got Sarah Beth into bed, she looked up at Josie. "My parents think I'm a lesbian because I'm not married with kids yet. If I were, I'd marry you. You are my favorite friend in the whole wide world, Jo. I love you."

"Oh no, things are good with Tom." Josie laughed. She did want to talk about Tom but also wanted to be funny. "Real good. We had crazy sex last night."

Sarah Beth sat up out of bed. "*What?*"

Josie laughed. "Kidding."

Sarah Beth lay back down and smiled. "I really like him for you. I'm sorry I didn't ask."

"It's okay."

"But no crazy sex?"

"Not yet."

"No nieces and nephews yet?" Sarah Beth smiled and rolled over onto her side.

"Not yet. Someday maybe but not yet."

Once Sarah Beth was asleep, Josie quietly snuck out the front door.

Sarah Beth was up early and went to work. She felt like an idiot for not allowing Shane to tell her his side of the story. She had taken a woman's word for it. A woman she didn't even know.

She decided she'd call Shane after work. She needed a good eight to ten hours to get him out of her skin, out of her mind.

But who was she kidding? She knew she couldn't get him out of her mind.

It was cold today. Thirty-seven degrees was the high.

She returned voice mails from parents.

Met with two children for disciplinary issues.

Made copies.

Made coffee.

Replied to more emails.

Cleaned out her inbox.

Looked at budgets.

Another reason she loved the holidays was that it was slower around work. She could take a breath. Get some air.

She also dreaded going home today. She knew she'd have to make a call she'd rather not make, but it was the right choice.

So, at six after six, she made it to her car. She'd driven today because it was indeed cold.

The rain started as just a tinkle against the roof and then a downpour.

She pulled out her phone. Clicked on Shane's number and called him.

"Sarah Beth," he said breathlessly.

She was certain the phone hadn't rung.

"Hey," she said awkwardly.

"Can I come over?" he asked.

No, no, he couldn't come over because then she'd see his face. Smell his smell. And wouldn't be able to be strong. If they did things over the phone, she might be able to hold her ground. Sarah Beth was no pushover.

"No. I can't, Shane." She swallowed the lump in her throat. "Why … why didn't you tell me?"

"I didn't know, Sarah Beth. I had no idea who Mia was until she showed up at my door that night."

"At your door that night? I'm not following."

Shane sighed into the phone. "She showed up the night before at my dad's place. Said I was the father. I-I didn't know what to do, Sarah Beth. She looked vaguely familiar. But I honest to God don't remember having sex with her."

"Go on."

"I planned to tell you that night at dinner. But thought better of it. Quite honestly, I was terrified I would break your heart … so I thought I'd tell you the next morning after breakfast. And then there she was."

The rain lightened up.

And she could vaguely hear the Christmas music from Main Street.

Sarah Beth wasn't sure what to say, except, "Is the baby yours?"

"Please don't hang up after you hear this."

Oh God. Her heart shook from her chest as her stomach met her ankles.

"I drove her into Eureka to get one of those DNA tests before the baby's here. I told her about you and about our past and everything. Told her that I was in love with you and that you have always been *the one.*"

Goddamn it, Sarah Beth's heart couldn't take much more. *The one?*

Stay strong, Sarah Beth. Stay strong.

Thank God he wasn't in front of her. Thank God she couldn't smell him or feel his skin.

"Look, I'm not sure where this puts us. I'll accept whatever you decide. But know this: you've always been *the one.*"

Sarah Beth didn't have many words for Shane because they were caught somewhere in her heart, and she wasn't sure how to get them out without crying, so she simply said, "I need some time, Shane."

"I know," he whispered. "I know."

The rain began again.

"I have to go." And with that, she hung up.

Sarah Beth didn't have closure. She had a few answers but no closure. *What would be her closure? What would be the final straw?* And then she asked herself the deepest, darkest question that she didn't have the answer to, *Would I stay with him if the baby is his?*

And on that cold, raining, wintery night, instead of drowning her heart in whiskey, she did what she loved. She went home and took out her little fake Christmas tree and her Christmas decorations. She put on Christmas music and began to decorate her little home.

Shane stayed in the back of her mind all night. He never left. In fact, she figured, he'd never left her heart since they were kids.

And as the evening crept on, her heart somehow felt fuller. Maybe it was the Christmas tree or the music or the decor. Or maybe it was hope.

It was the feeling Shane gave her.

Shane made her feel like the most important person in the room.

As if he loved her heart more than he loved his own.

As if he would take care of her and keep her safe.

As if he'd loved her far longer than she loved him, but he had just been too scared to say anything.

Now, she knew.

Shane Sawyer was in love with Sarah Beth Dawson.

Because, at the end of the night, as she stared at the twinkling lights on her Christmas tree and before she tucked herself in bed, she asked herself one question for the final time.

If Shane is the father, would I be willing to stay?

TEN

Shane had felt a broken heart before only once—when his mom died.

Even at ten years old, he couldn't figure out why his chest hurt so bad. Why it was hard to breathe. Why he felt so lonely. All he wanted was for all of this to go away and for everything to go back to normal. At age ten, Shane's eyes were so swollen from all the crying he had done at night, in the shower, in the barn when he took care of the calves.

He didn't dare cry in front of his father. It wasn't that he was scared of what would happen; it was just that he didn't want to make his dad sadder than he already was.

So, after a week of all that grief nonsense, Shane had convinced himself that all the crying and sadness weren't going to bring his mom back, so he'd better stop carrying on and pull his shit together.

The current situation was no different. Seventeen years later, his chest hurt. It was hard to breathe. And all he wanted was for things to go back to normal.

But this time?

He didn't cry.

He swallowed every last ounce of his decision not to tell Sarah Beth about Mia immediately.

Shane's mom's death had been out of his control.

But he sure as hell could have prevented this one.

What Shane wouldn't give to go back, to rewind time.

He'd sat at her front porch for two hours. Knocked. Pounded. Waited for her to at least give him some sign that she was all right.

When she didn't, Shane called Josie.

He'd told her everything.

Told her he just wanted someone to check on Sarah Beth. Make sure she was all right.

But at some point in his life, he had to start making the right decisions for the right reasons and not the wrong decisions for what felt right.

Shane played that tape back in his head from some months ago in Texas.

Tried to remember Mia's face. Some recollection that they'd had sex.

If he had drunk so much.

Allowed himself to indulge.

Remembered to put a condom on.

In the circuit, there are women everywhere. Beautiful women.

Pearly white teeth.

Big smiles.

Long hair.

Short hair.

But to Shane, it didn't matter. He felt the regret in his bones. Played the *if I had just* game in his head countless times.

But facts were facts.

They'd have the results in two weeks. Two days before Christmas. Two weeks was a long time to wait when life got flipped upside down.

He'd just have to wait patiently and pray to God that Sarah Beth would take him back. At least give them a chance. If the kid was his, then he'd take full responsibility. He'd love his kid, just like his dad loved him. His mom loved him.

"Hey, you want to come out here? Need your help." His dad peeked in through his bedroom door.

Shane stood. "Yeah."

He knew his dad could see his pain, see his son grappling with big decisions that lay ahead, but he tried to hide it anyway.

Shane followed his dad out to the living room.

Jack Sawyer, the man who had sworn off Christmas when Shane's mom died, had set up a Christmas tree in the corner of their living room. Hung two stockings on the mantel, next to his mom's ashes.

Shane didn't know what to say, but in that moment, he felt his mom. He felt every part of her in the room with them that night. It was the first time in seventeen years that he might just enjoy a tiny ounce of Christmas.

"Dad …" Shane searched for the right words as the pressure in his chest let up just a little.

"I'm sorry, son. I should have done this a long time ago. I denied you some of what could have been the best times in our lives because I couldn't see what was right in front of me. This sweet little boy, thinking Christmas was just another workday. It's not." He paused. Stared down at the carpet. "Don't let your grief dictate who you are. Whether you figure it out with Sarah Beth or not, don't let your broken heart dictate the rest of your life. Because I did. I missed out on you as a kid." His dad placed a fist to his mouth to hide his expression as the tears welled up in his eyes. "Son, no matter what, I'm always going to be there for you. And I promise, the outcome of this situation, I'll be the best damn grandpa in the world."

Shane's words got caught in his throat. He didn't know what to say or what to do, but he'd never seen his father be so open with his emotions before.

"Help me with the lights outside?" his dad asked.

Shane smiled. He'd always wanted to put lights on the house. But they never did. At Christmas, their house was lit with only a dim torchlight and a whole lot of sadness.

"Thanks," Shane said. "Thank you, Dad."

And with that, the two men who'd spent years running from each other and from the pain of loss and the pain of Christmas started to create new traditions built on love.

They stood back and admired their work. Two thousand twinkling, colorful bulbs, four big lawn ornaments, and a giant Santa on the roof, and they were done.

"God, I forgot how much I enjoyed Christmas," his dad said.

"You enjoyed Christmas?"

Jack looked at his son curiously. "Don't you remember us doing this same thing before your mom died?"

"No." Shane shook his head and thought real hard, trying to recall the memories that had been locked away for so long. But in that moment, Shane realized that he'd spent years trying to forget things, so the pain didn't hurt so bad. He'd stuffed all the good things away, so he wouldn't remember because when he did, his chest grew heavy, and the sadness returned. So, on that day, when he was ten years old and made the choice to stop hurting, he'd also made an unconscious choice to forget the good too.

When they walked back to the front door, there was a small gift in red wrapping paper. On the tag, it said, *To my boys.*

"Did you put that there?" Shane's dad asked.

"No. Did you?"

Jack shook his head. Reached down and picked up the small gift. Handed it to his son. "Here, you open it."

Shane took it and unwrapped it.

Inside was a small framed picture of Shane at about six years old and his dad, arm in arm with grins on Christmas Day, in the front yard with all the Christmas lawn ornaments, Santa on the roof. His mother had obviously taken the photo.

A note fell out.

Shane and his dad were dumbfounded.

Shane asked his dad, "You didn't do this?"

Jack shook his head. "No. And you didn't?"

Shane shook his head.

LITTLE WHITE CHRISTMAS

Shane bent down and picked up the note.

I'm here. You just can't see me.

Love,
Mom

Chills ran the length of Shane's spine.

He looked at his dad, his mouth open.

Jack was no different. Neither of them said anything. They just stood and stared at the note and then each other for enough time to realize what had happened.

Finally, Jack rubbed his face with his hand. "We aren't dreaming, right?"

Shane looked at his dad and began to giggle and then laugh. And so did his dad.

"I have an idea." He pulled his phone from his front pocket. "Come on."

His dad followed him to the spot where they'd taken the photo twenty-one years ago. Shane held up his phone. He put his arm around his dad, and his dad did the same. With tears in both their eyes, they smiled, and Shane took the picture.

That night, Shane was truthful to his dad about what was really going on with his shoulder.

The outlook wasn't good, but it was better than the alternative. He couldn't live with the lies anymore. He'd lied to protect his dad, his dreams for his son. And a lot of it was also that he was too scared to see the truth.

But what was truth in lies?

He'd read somewhere that a clean conscience made for a soft pillow.

It had been thirteen days, almost two weeks. Three days before Christmas. Shane had given Sarah Beth time, as Josie had suggested.

It just about killed him.

In that thirteen days, he learned to slow down. He followed the doctor's orders.

Dad finally hired two ranch hands to help pick up the slack. Shane didn't like it, but he had to accept it.

Mia went back to Texas.

The clinic said they'd put the results in the mail.

Because Shane was on a new playing field now with right decisions, he'd started a letter for Sarah Beth on his phone. He told her about his shoulder and the truth of it all. He told her about his mom and the memories he had with her and the gift she'd given him and his dad. He told her about what it felt like when he thought about leaving the pro-rodeo circuit. He told her about how he loved the way she was superstitious and how she loved Christmas and how he was surprised that the whole damn world hadn't fallen in love with the dimple she had just below her mouth. He told her that he missed her body and how being in love and walking away were two of the hardest things he'd ever experienced. He also told her that he'd wait for as long as it took to win her back. That he wasn't going anywhere. He told her about a few job opportunities that might require some travel. That Justin Boots, a western footwear company, had called and asked him to do several commercials for them. That Wrangler had asked if he'd be the spokesperson for the following year. And the contract was pretty hefty, but he hadn't told Sarah Beth about that part. He knew she wouldn't care.

When Shane started to get truly honest about who he was and what he'd done and righted his wrongs, things began to happen.

He received job opportunities beyond his wildest dreams.

Sometimes, people fell into the right things at the right time.

Shane checked the mail on his way home, and inside the mailbox was the letter he'd been waiting for. He wanted to throw up and burn it, but at the same time, he wanted to rip it open.

He took the mail inside, and his dad was in the kitchen.

Jack knew immediately that something was wrong. "What is it?"

Shane tossed the mail down on the counter. "The results of the paternity test came."

Jack paused. Set the milk jug down on the counter.

Jack had decided to stop drinking. It had been almost thirteen days since his last drink. Jack might have been a heavy drinker, maybe a functioning alcoholic, but he knew he had to leave it in the past with his grief.

But Shane and Jack couldn't keep enough milk and candy in the house. For whatever reason, those were two of Jack's weaknesses at the moment. Shane would take that any day.

They both stared down at the letter with the return address as LACO Laboratories.

Jack finally spoke, "Whatever it is, son, it will be okay. And if Sarah Beth can accept you as you and maybe your unborn child, then she's in it for all the right reasons."

Shane nodded and looked down at the envelope and back to his dad. "I'm scared I'm going to lose her forever."

Jack shrugged. "You could. But it will still be okay."

Jack knew what he was talking about. He'd lived it.

With that, Shane took the letter and began to open it, his stomach in knots.

ELEVEN

Sarah Beth

I t had been thirteen days since Sarah Beth had spoken to Shane.

And she'd felt every single hour.

So, when she picked up her phone and heard the tone of his voice, her heart grew warm, her knees grew weak, and her hands grew clammy.

"Hey. Can we talk in person?" he asked.

It was cold in Dillon Creek.

Colder than usual. Even for December.

And Sarah Beth had superstitions about that.

Before she answered him, she grabbed her wool coat, her scarf and gloves, and her purse. "Where?" she asked, just as breathless.

"The Christmas tree?"

She nodded, though he couldn't see it. She knew she'd made her decision, and he'd have to accept it.

It will all be okay, right? she'd asked herself several times throughout each day that passed in the last two weeks. *It would have to be.*

It was just getting dark.

The hustle and bustle of Main Street on Christmas made her heart less tender. In fact, it filled with some joy a little.

The cold nipped at her face, and her stomach was full of butterflies. She made her way to the Christmas tree at the end of Main Street.

The Christmas music played.

She watched families across the street. To the Dillon Creek Repertory Theater for a showing of *A Christmas Story*.

She watched people through windows as she passed by.

Sarah Beth walked quickly, and when she saw Shane Sawyer standing in front of the gigantic tree, she felt her heart almost stop.

The way he looked, his down jacket to his piercing moss-colored eyes, strong jawline, and his five o'clock shadow.

The way he stood.

Sarah Beth slowly approached him. "Hey," she meekly said.

Shane looked at Sarah Beth. His eyes lit up. "Hey."

She heard the relief in his voice. She saw the compassion in his eyes. She saw the love he had for her.

Shane was nervous. She could tell because he kept taking his hands in and out of his pockets. Instead of watching him do this one more time, she took his hands in hers.

He finally said, "I received the results from the paternity test today." He rushed the words out, as if it were a bad memory or bad news.

Sarah Beth swallowed hard. Tried to keep her smile. She didn't say anything. She just waited and held her breath.

"The baby isn't mine."

And without missing a beat, Sarah Beth pulled Shane into her arms and whispered in his ear, "Even if the baby were yours, I would have married you anyway."

Shane pulled away. His eyes wide.

Shane kissed Sarah Beth hard and deep and held her as close as he could with a big coat on.

Everything around them disappeared.

The Christmas tree.

Main Street.

The season.

The people.

They became drunk on love, on each other. And Sarah Beth knew in her heart that this Shane Sawyer had been *the one* all along.

They kissed again and again until they drew a small crowd.

And when Sarah Beth and Shane finally noticed, the crowd began to clap.

Jack had tears in his eyes.

Why is Jack here?

Shane whispered, "He's been doing that a lot lately."

Sarah Beth's parents watched. Her mother high-fived her dad and the people around them.

Wait. Why are my parents here?

Josie and Tom watched. Giving a thumbs-up to Sarah Beth, Josie was holding back tears. Tom held her close.

Why is everyone watching us?

Delveen yelled, "It's about time!"

Pearl laughed.

Mabe rolled her eyes.

Erla smiled.

And Clyda covered her mouth.

But when Sarah Beth turned back to Shane, he was on one knee, shaking like a leaf.

"Sarah Beth."

She covered her mouth as the tears welled in her eyes too. *Oh, God.*

"Before our family and friends, in your favorite season, by your favorite Christmas tree, in your favorite town, with our favorite people, I just need to tell you that you've always been *the one.* Since we were kids, I knew you were the only one. The way you looked at me, you saw past my exterior and right to my insides. I watched you from afar, terrified to take the chance. I've made some poor choices in my life, but you're the best one I've ever made." Shane stopped. Caught his breath. "Sarah Beth Dawson, will you marry me?"

The crowd gasped.

Sarah Beth knew two things for sure: she was absolutely in love with Shane Sawyer, and she was willing to take the chance.

She nodded and held her own tears back. "*Yes!*"

Shane put the ring on her finger, and he stood.

Sarah Beth grabbed ahold of him and kissed him with everything she could.

The crowd clapped and cheered.

Later that night, as the town gathered down Main Street for the annual tractor parade, Sarah Beth's hand tightly in Shane's, she asked, "How did all those people know?"

Shane kissed her temple as her back rested against his front while people walked over to congratulate them. "I invited them."

Sarah Beth turned to look up at Shane.

He shrugged. "I knew you'd want them to be a part of that more than anything."

"But why were The Ladybugs there?"

Shane laughed. "I have no idea."

Sarah Beth laughed at Delveen's and Pearl's ability to find out news before anyone.

"I asked your parents for your hand in marriage after I got the results of the paternity test. Regardless of what you might say, I couldn't leave here without taking the chance."

Shane pulled her close to him from the small of her back. He kissed her softly and then more urgently. She groaned in his mouth.

"Oh, Ms. Dawson, you can't do that here. You're going to break this cowboy."

But the tractor parade was Sarah Beth's favorite event of the year in Dillon Creek, and she couldn't miss it. They couldn't miss it.

The fire whistle sounded, indicating the beginning of the parade.

Sarah Beth gave one last kiss to her fiancé, and she turned to face Main Street among her family and dear friends.

This time, it didn't matter if she stood on the crack in the sidewalk, wished someone happy birthday before the big day, faced mirrors and hell, drove straight home after a funeral, or saw her breath in November instead of December. Because the storm that had blown into her life that day was the only storm she'd fallen in love with, and she knew they'd live happily ever after.

TWELVE

"Did you see that Sarah Beth and Shane's engagement was on the front page of the *Dillon Creek Echo*?" Clyda held up the newspaper. "What a love story."

Erla chimed in, "Sounds like another love story we know." She bumped her old friend. "Colt and Anna."

Clyda smiled. "Yes, that one too."

Delveen started, "Well, you know what I heard? I heard that Tess and Casey are back together. Go figure. All the way up in Ketchikan, Alaska, they found their way back to each other."

They all stared at Clyda Atwood.

"How would I know? I'm just the old lady in the family. They don't tell me shit."

But Clyda knew. She knew the whole story. She knew her grandson loved Tess Morgan with all his heart even if he never said it, even if he was willing to walk away from riding bulls for her. But time and memories changed people. She just prayed they'd figure it out together even if it meant mending bridges with the Morgan family. After all, Christmas was all about forgiveness and peace. She just hoped they found it before it was too late.

"Anyway, what story will you tell us next after Tess and Casey, Delveen? Because you know all the gossip. The story about Cash and Scarlet?" Mabe asked.

But instead of looking at Delveen, they looked at Erla. Scarlet was Erla's granddaughter. The comment surprised Erla, coming from Mabe. Erla knew Scarlet and Cash Atwood had spent time together as kids. But he was reckless in his decision-making. A bit of a loose cannon. Surely, Scarlet would think that through.

Why on earth didn't my granddaughter mention Cash when she came to town? Erla thought. *How does Mabe know something I don't?*

"Why would you ask that, Mabe?" came from Erla's mouth before she could really think it through.

Mabe cocked her head to the right. "You're the one who told me, Erla."

Erla was clearly confused, and so was Mabe.

Had she told Mabe she'd heard or seen something? She couldn't remember.

Mabe must have seen the look of fear on Erla's face because she said, "Well, maybe it wasn't you."

But it had been. Erla and Mabe had been friends for far too long for the look she'd had to go unnoticed.

Merry, one of the owners of The Rusty Nail, approached the table. "All ready, ladies? Here's the tab. Let me know if I can get you anything else."

Erla, Clyda, Delveen, Pearl, and Mabe made their way out of The Rusty Nail and went their separate ways.

"Mabe"—Erla looked around as the group dispersed— "did I tell you that? About Scarlet and Cash?"

Mabe was nervous for her friend, but she knew she'd better tell Erla Brockmeyer the truth. Ever since Mabe's incident with the shopping and the alcohol, they'd promised to always tell each other the truth. "Yes. Right after Scarlet left after Don's funeral. You don't remember?"

Erla clearly didn't. Concern grew in her stomach like a cancer.

"It was just the grief, Erla. Be gentle with yourself, all right?" Mabe touched Erla's shoulder.

Yes, it could have been the grief. Yes, it could. It most likely was.

She laughed. "You're probably right."

But deep down, Erla knew something was awfully wrong.

EPILOGUE

"Come on, babe." Shane took Sarah Beth's hand and led her outside to her front yard after he'd put the blindfold on her.

It was Christmas Day after all. And they could only enjoy that day for another few hours.

They faced Sarah Beth's small house, and Shane removed the blindfold.

"It's freezing out here, Shane. P-p-please, let's go back inside, where it's warm."

"Just one last surprise," he said.

After they'd made love for the third time that day, Sarah Beth had fallen asleep. He'd taken the liberty to drive down to Nelson's Feed and buy all the lawn ornaments and Christmas lights they had in stock.

"Okay, open your eyes."

When Sarah Beth opened her eyes, she couldn't believe how many lawn ornaments were on her lawn, and it looked like her house could be seen from space. Her heart rejoiced, and she smiled and looked at Shane as she took him in her arms and kissed him. "I love it. It's so perfect."

Shane pulled out his phone. "Okay, let's take a picture. Maybe this could be our tradition. Christmas night photo."

Sarah Beth remembered when Shane had mentioned the picture his mom took of him and his dad at night among the lawn ornaments and Christmas lights.

Sarah Beth and Shane both smiled big, cheesy smiles and laughed.

And when they looked through photos, his breath hitched.

"What is it?" Sarah Beth asked. "Are you all right?"

"There." Shane pointed at the outline in the background.

At first, it looked like maybe a reflection of one of the many, many, many lights Shane had put out.

But it wasn't at all.

It was an outline of a woman, almost ghostlike, which looked just like Shane's mom, Corinne, beaming at the two of them.

It was said that, sometimes, the universe could pull a fantastic magic trick.

The lighting had to be just right.

The season needed to be perfect.

Joy must exist.

Hearts must be full and good.

And if all this happened at the same exact time, miracles would reveal themselves at the moments their loved ones needed them most.

Always believe in miracles.

The End

ACKNOWLEDGMENTS

I wrote *Little White Christmas* because readers had asked me when *Saving Tess* would be coming out. The truth was, I didn't know. But I wanted to give my readers something to hold on to until then.

I wrote this novella in a week and a half, but that's just the beginning of the work that needs to be done to produce a book in this world. There's a lot of behind-the-scenes work that has to be accomplished to put the book in readers' hands.

First, I'd like to thank my incredible editor and formatter for squeezing my work in at the last minute. Jovana, you are incredible at what you do, and I'm so grateful to have you on my team.

Second, a huge thank you to Tash Drake at Outlined With Love Designs for the beautiful book cover. I was speechless when I received the cover.

Third, thank you to Taylor Colbert Kelley for help with the blurb for *Little White Christmas* and all the moral support. You are truly a gem, and I'm so lucky to be on this writing journey with you.

Fourth, to my readers—Without you all, this little novella wouldn't be here.

Last, to my family—Thank you for being my soft place to land.

A NOTE TO THE READER

THANK YOU FOR READING *LITTLE WHITE CHRISTMAS.*

If you enjoyed the book, please consider leaving an honest review on the website where you purchased the book. By leaving a review, it makes the book visible to more readers. The more reviews, the better promotional opportunities for the author.

Get the latest information on book releases, sales, and more.

Sign up for J. Lynn Bailey's newsletter at http://bit.ly/2VVmqna to get sneak peeks, early excerpts, and free books.

Have you joined my reading group, The Bailey Bunch, at http://bit.ly/2EscfjT? Join for behind-the-scenes looks, giveaways, and top-secret book information. Learn about the inner workings of my writing process and my crazy ideas.

CONNECT WITH J. LYNN ONLINE

www.facebook.com/AuthorJLynnBailey

www.instagram.com/jlynnbaileybooks

www.jlynnbaileybooks.com

ABOUT THE AUTHOR

J. Lynn Bailey is an award-winning and best-selling author who has loved to write since she learned to read around the second grade. She earned a bachelor's degree and master's degree from Humboldt State University.

When she isn't running her children to their next sporting event, watching *North Woods Law,* or on the hunt for her next Laffy Taffy joke, you can probably find her holed up in her writing room, feverishly working on her next book. She lives in Northern California with her family.

OTHER BOOKS BY J. LYNN BAILEY

THE GRANITE HARBOR SERIES

Peony Red
Violet Ugly
Magnolia Road
Lilies on Main

THE DILLON CREEK SERIES

Taking Anna

STAND-ALONES

Standing Sideways
The Light We See
Black Five